Prometheus Bound

DOVER · THRIFT · EDITIONS

Prometheus Bound

AESCHYLUS

TRANSLATED BY
GEORGE THOMSON

DOVER PUBLICATIONS, INC.
New York

DOVER THRIFT EDITIONS

GENERAL EDITOR: STANLEY APPELBAUM
EDITOR OF THIS VOLUME: ALAN WEISSMAN

Performance

This Dover Thrift Edition may be used in its entirety, in adaptation or in any other way for theatrical productions, professional and amateur, in the United States, without fee, permission or acknowledgment. (This may not apply outside of the United States, as copyright conditions may vary.)

Copyright

Bibliographical Note

This Dover edition, first published in 1995, is an unabridged republication of the English translation by George Thomson, M.A., as it appeared in *Aeschylus, The Prometheus Bound*, edited by George Thomson, first published by the Cambridge University Press, Cambridge, England, 1932. A new introductory Note has been specially prepared for this edition.

Library of Congress Cataloging-in-Publication Data

Aeschylus.
    [Prometheus bound. English]
    Prometheus bound / Aeschylus ; translated by George Thomson.
       p.   cm. — (Dover thrift editions)
    ISBN 0-486-28762-9
    1. Prometheus (Greek mythology)—Drama. I. Thomson, George Derwent. II. Title. III. Series.
PA3827.P8T5   1995
882′.01—dc20

                                            95-49133
                                          CIP

Manufactured in the United States of America
Dover Publications, Inc., 31 East 2nd Street, Mineola, N.Y. 11501

Note

If anyone may be said to have "invented" the kind of drama we know as Greek tragedy, it was Aeschylus (525–456 B.C.). The drama he wrote, like that of his predecessors, was derived from choral song and dance and played an important role in the religious and cultural life of the Athenian community. Yet, besides the chorus, only one actor had appeared in a given scene in early Greek tragedy. Aeschylus' stroke of genius was to add a second actor, thereby vastly increasing the dramatic possibilities.

The next generation brought the great dramatists Sophocles and Euripides, who added further refinements. With the surviving plays of these three — and there are only 32 such plays — we have all the complete examples left to us of one of the greatest and most influential arts of Western civilization. The *Prometheus Bound*, believed to be one of the last of Aeschylus' plays (only seven complete plays by him survive), was the first play of a trilogy — that is, three connected plays performed on the same day. Although, unfortunately, only this first play of the Prometheus trilogy has survived, it is by itself a major contribution to the dramatic literature.

Prometheus was a son of the first generation of Titans, a superhuman race. The Olympian god Zeus, son of Cronos, was the ruler of the earth at the time the play represents. The great crime of Prometheus, on which the play looks back, was that of having bestowed upon the mortal race of humans the gift of fire, hitherto reserved for the immortals, and, with it, all the arts of civilization. For this Zeus condemns Prometheus to being chained to a rock forever, with worse punishments to come for his obstinacy in refusing to repent his deed. Eventually, Prometheus is freed — as Aeschylus' audience would have known before seeing the play. His release, however, is not dramatized until the next play in the trilogy, now lost. But — this was true of Greek drama in general — the purpose of *Prometheus Bound* was not to surprise the audience with a trick ending, but to immerse it in a vivid depiction of the hero's situation and in the emotions that arise from it. This purpose Aeschylus achieved with his typical grace and magnificence, demonstrating why the ancients named him "Father of Tragedy."

This English translation, by George Thomson, is sufficiently clear as to require little annotation. Possibly unfamiliar to some readers are the terms "strophe," "antistrophe" and "epode." These are parts of the choral ode that was one of the components of Greek tragedy. Each type of verse was accompanied by its own kind of dance step. In the antistrophe, the chorus moved in the direction opposite to that of the strophe. The strophe and antistrophe were frequently, though not always, followed by an epode, the concluding portion of a choral ode.

Prometheus Bound

Characters

Prometheus, *a Titan*.

Io

Hermes, *messenger of Zeus*.

Hephaestus, *god of fire*.

Oceanus, *god of the ocean*.

Might

Violence

Chorus of Oceanids (*daughters of Oceanus*).

Prometheus Bound

(*Enter* PROMETHEUS, *escorted by* MIGHT *and* VIOLENCE, *and accompanied by* HEPHAESTUS, *who carries the implements of his craft*)

MIGHT

> To Earth's far-distant confines we are come,
> The tract of Scythia, waste untrod by man.
>   And now, Hephaestus, thou must mind the task
> Ordained thee by the Father — to enchain
> This malefactor on yon mountain crags
> In indissoluble bands of adamant.
> Thy flower, fount of the arts, the light of fire,
> He stole and gave to mortals. Such the sin
> For which he must make recompense to heaven,
> And so be taught to accept the tyranny
> Of Zeus, and check his charity to man.

HEPHAESTUS

> O Might, and Violence, for you the word
> Of Zeus hath been fulfilled — your part is done.
> But I have not the heart by force to bind
> A god, my kinsman, in this wintry glen.
> And yet I must brazen myself to do it; ·
> For grave it is to scant the Father's word.

True-counselling Themis' lofty-ambitioned Son,
Not by my will, nor thine, shall rigorous bonds
Imprison thee in this unpeopled waste,
Where neither mortal form shall greet thine eye
Nor voice thine ear, but, parched in the sun's pure flame,
Thy beauty's bloom shall perish. Welcome to thee
Shall starry-kirtled Night enshroud the day,
Welcome the sun dispel the frosts of dawn;
And the anguish of thy state shall gnaw thy heart
For ever — unborn is thy deliverer.
    Such thy reward for charity to man:
A god, thou didst defy the wrath of gods,
On men their powers bestowing unrighteously.
So on this cheerless rock must thou stand guard,
Upright, unsleeping, unbending the knee,
And with many a groan of unavailing grief
Cry out. Implacable is the heart of Zeus,
And harsh is every king whose power is new.

MIGHT

Enough: why this delay? why waste your pity?
Do you not hate the god all gods abhor,
Betrayer of your privilege to man?

HEPHAESTUS

The tie of kin and comradeship is strange.

MIGHT

True, but is't possible to disregard
The Father's word? do you not revere that more?

HEPHAESTUS

Ah, you were ever pitiless and proud!

MIGHT

> To grieve for *him* cures nothing; so do you
> Labour no more where labour is in vain.

HEPHAESTUS

> O most abhorrent handicraft of mine!

MIGHT

> Why do you hate it? In plain truth, your art
> Is guiltless of the work that's now to do.

HEPHAESTUS

> Yet would that it had fallen to another!

MIGHT

> All things are troublesome, save to rule the gods:
> Liberty is the privilege of Zeus.

HEPHAESTUS (*pointing to chains*)

> These teach me that, and I can make no answer.

MIGHT

> No more delay then — in these chains bind *him*,
> For fear the Father see your faltering.

HEPHAESTUS

> Here are the curb-chains, ready to my hand.

MIGHT

> Then manacle his hands with all your might,
> Uplift the hammer, strike, and nail him down!

HEPHAESTUS

> See, 'tis not vain, the work proceeds apace.

MIGHT

    Strike harder, pin him, leave no fetter loose.
    His wit can circumvent the closest strait.

HEPHAESTUS

    That arm is fixed, fastened inextricably.

MIGHT

    And now encase the other, that he may learn,
    For all his craft, he is no match for Zeus.

HEPHAESTUS

    Of none, save him, have I deserved reproach.

MIGHT

    Now drive this stubborn adamantine edge
    Deep through his breast and nail it firmly down.

HEPHAESTUS

    Aiai, Prometheus! — for *thy* pains I groan.

MIGHT

    Once more you falter, weeping for the foes
    Of Zeus. Beware lest you should need your pity.

HEPHAESTUS

    The spectacle thou seest doth wound the eye.

MIGHT

    A knave I see repaid with his deserts.
    Come, cast this iron girth about his ribs.

HEPHAESTUS

    It must be done, you need not shout me on.

MIGHT

And yet I *will* shout — ay, I will hound you on.
Step down. Enclose his ankles in these rings.

HEPHAESTUS

See, without length of labour, it is done.

MIGHT

Now thrust these penetrating spancels home,
For hard it is to please our taskmaster.

HEPHAESTUS

How like your looks the utterance of your tongue!

MIGHT

Be soft yourself, so please you, but do not chide
My stubborn spirit and temperament severe.

HEPHAESTUS

His feet are netted. Let us go our ways. (*Exit*)

MIGHT

Here now wax proud and plunder powers divine —
Thy gifts to creatures of a day! How can
Mortals relieve thee in thy present state?
Falsely we named thee the Foresighted One,
Prometheus — thine the need of foresight now,
How from *this* art to extricate *thyself*!

(*Exeunt* MIGHT *and* VIOLENCE)

PROMETHEUS

O divine Sky, and swiftly-winging Breezes,
O River-springs, and multitudinous gleam
Of smiling Ocean — to thee, All-Mother Earth,

And to the Sun's all-seeing orb I cry:
See what I suffer from the gods, a god!

    Witness how with anguish broken
    Through ages of time without number
    I shall labour in agony. Such are the bonds
    That the new-throned Lord of the Blest hath designed
    For my shame and dishonour.
    Pheu, pheu! for the pain that is now and to come
    I groan, and I cry, where is the destined
    Term of my trial and my travail?

And yet what say I? All things I foreknow
That are to be: no unforeseen distress
Shall visit me, and I must bear the will
Of Fate as lightly as I may, and learn
The invincible strength of Necessity.
Yet of my present state I cannot speak,
Cannot be silent. The gifts I gave to man
Have harnessed me beneath this harsh duress.
I hunted down the stealthy fount of fire
In fennel stored, which schooled the race of men
In every art and taught them great resource.
Such the transgression which I expiate,
A helpless captive, shackled, shelterless!

Ah ah, ea ea!
    What echo, what fragrance unseen wingeth nigh me?
Is it divine or mortal, or of mingled blood?
    Visiting this desolate edge of earth,
Spectator of my agony — with what purpose else?

Behold in chains confined an ill-starred god,
The detested of Zeus and rejected of all
The celestial band that assembleth aloft
In the heavenly courts of the Highest,
For my too great love of the children of men!
Pheu, pheu! what again is the murmur I hear
As of birds hard by?
And the air is astir with the whispering beat
Of their hurrying wings.
Oh, fearful is all that approacheth.

CHORUS OF OCEANIDS (*Strophe 1*)
O be not fearful — as a friend in flight contending to this
rock my airy voyage have I winged.
Eager for this adventure, my father's leave hardly I won.
Swiftly I rode on the flying breezes.
I heard afar off the reverberating echoes in my hollow cave,
and unflushed with the shame of maidens
I sped on my chariot-steed unsandalled.

PROMETHEUS
Aiai, aiai!
Daughters of Tethys, the bride many-childed of
Oceanus, who with unslumbering tides
Doth encompass the earth,
Bear witness, behold how cruelly bound
And enchained in a wild and precipitous glen
I shall keep my disconsolate vigil!

CHORUS (*Antistrophe 1*)
I see, Prometheus, and a mist of grief descendeth on my
vision, tears are springing to my eyes

Thus to behold thy beauty by day and night blasted in
   these
Adamant shackles of shame and torment.
For new the rulers who are throned above in heaven, and
   the laws of Zeus are new, framed for a harsh domin-
   ion.
The mighty of old he hath brought to nothing.

PROMETHEUS

O would in the boundless abyss of the earth,
Bottomless Tartarus,
Where Hades doth welcome the souls of the dead,
In invincible bondage my body were crushed,
That nor god nor another might mock my estate!
But here I am hung as a plaything of storms
And a mark for my enemies' laughter!

CHORUS (*Strophe* 2)

What god is he so hard of heart that such a spectacle could
   delight?
Who doth not share thy sufferings, save Zeus? For in his
   spirit is no pity. Inflexibly
Fixed on vengeance, still his wrath smiteth the Sons of the
   Sky; ay, and shall not soften
Till his heart have its fill of revenge, or a mightier
Hand from him plunder his stolen kingdom.

PROMETHEUS

Yet of me, yet of me, though battered and bent,
Limb-pierced by his shackles of insolent wrong,
Shall the prince who presideth in heaven have need,
To reveal him the new-found plan whereby

Of his sceptre and sway he shall be stripped bare.
And then I, unappeased by his charms honey-tongued
And unmoved by his merciless threats, will withhold
From him all that I know, till he grant me release
From the bonds that encompass my limbs and atone
For the shameful disgrace that I suffer.

CHORUS (*Antistrophe 2*)

Nay, *thou* art bold and dost not bow before thy keen adversities,
And too unbridled is thy tongue. I tremble, and my spirit is a-quiver with a piercing fear,
With terror for thy future state, when is it fated for thee rest from these thy labours
To behold? Unapproachable, hard to appease is the
Heart in the breast of the Son of Cronos.

PROMETHEUS

Full well do I know he is harsh and a law
To himself, but in time, notwithstanding, I ween,
Crushed by this danger, his heart shall be humbled,
And, becalming his irreconcilable rage,
He shall hasten to union and friendship with me
Eagerly, eagerly waited.

CHORUS

All things unveil, make manifest to us
Upon what pretext seizing thee doth Zeus
Outrage thee with such agony and shame?
Teach us, unless to speak should bring thee harm.

PROMETHEUS
>Painful it is for me to speak of this,
Painful is silence — 'tis misery every way.

As soon as war among the gods began
And strife internal broke the peace of heaven,
Some eager to cast Cronos from his throne
That Zeus might reign, and others contrary
Intent that Zeus should never rule the gods,
Then I, though wise the counsel that I pressed
Upon the Titans, Sons of Heaven and Earth,
Could win no hearing. All my cunning wiles
Counting as nought, in arrogance of heart
They hoped by force for easy mastery.
But often I had heard my mother, Earth
And Themis, one form under many names,
Predict the future as it would come to pass,
How not by strength nor by the stouter hand,
By guile alone the reigning powers would fall.
Such was the tale they heard revealed by me
But deemed unworthy even of a glance.

And then, it seemed, my best remaining choice
Was, with my mother's aid, to take my stand
Where help was welcome, at the side of Zeus;
And through my counsels in the nether gloom
Of Tartarus ancestral Cronos lies
With all his comrades. Such are the services
I rendered to the tyrant of the gods,
And these cruel penalties are my reward.
For tyranny, it seems, is never free
From this distemper — faithlessness to friends.

But to your question, on what pretext he

Outrages me thus, I will now reply.
No sooner was he on his father's throne
Seated secure than he assigned the gods
Their several privileges, to each appointing
Powers, but held the hapless race of man
Of no account, resolving to destroy
All human kind and sow new seed on earth.
And none defied his will in this save me,
I dared to do it, I delivered man
From death and steep destruction. Such the crime
For which I pay with these fell agonies,
Painful to suffer, pitiful to see.
For pitying man in preference to myself
I am debarred from pity; and thus I stand
Tortured, to Zeus a spectacle of shame.

CHORUS

Oh, iron-hearted he and wrought of stone,
Whoe'er, Prometheus, grieveth not for thy
Calamities — a sight I never hoped
To see, and now behold with broken heart.

PROMETHEUS

Ay, to my friends, I *am* a sight for pity.

CHORUS

Canst thou perchance have carried thy daring further?

PROMETHEUS

I stayed man from foreknowledge of his fate.

CHORUS

And what cure for that malady didst thou find?

PROMETHEUS

First, I implanted in his heart blind hopes.

CHORUS

A blessing, truly, hast thou given to man.

PROMETHEUS

And furthermore, I bestowed fire upon him.

CHORUS

Have creatures of a day the flame of fire?

PROMETHEUS

They have, and many arts shall learn therefrom.

CHORUS

Such then the accusation whereon Zeus—

PROMETHEUS

Outrages me and ceases not from wrong.

CHORUS

What, is no end appointed for thy labours?

PROMETHEUS

No end, save when *he* thinks it meet to end them.

CHORUS

When will he? Oh, what hope? Dost thou not see
That thou hast sinned? And yet that word gives me
No pleasure, and pains thee. Let us dismiss
Such thoughts, and from thy labours seek release.

PROMETHEUS

Easy for him who keeps his foot outside
The miry clay to give advice to one

In trouble. All this was known to me:
I willed to sin, I willed it, I confess.
My help to man brought suffering to myself.
Not that I thought that with such pains as these
I would be wasted on precipitous heights,
The tenant of this solitary rock.
But for my present sorrows mourn no more,
Step down to earth and to my future fortunes
Give ear and learn all things from end to end.
O hearken to me, hearken, take compassion
On him who suffers now, for, ever-restless,
Trouble alights on one now, then another.

CHORUS

    To thy eager appeal will thy hearers respond
    Gladly, Prometheus.
    Lo, fleet-footed I step down from my wind-
    Swift seat on the ways of the fowls of the air
    And alight on the chill earth, eager to hark
    To the tale full-told of thy labours.

(*Enter* OCEANUS, *mounted on a sea-horse*)

OCEANUS

    To the end of my long journey, Prometheus,
    Am I come, from afar have I travelled to thee,
    Mounted on this wing-swift bird who is quick
    To obey my command without bridle or bit;
    And in this thy affliction, believe me, I share.
    For indeed I am drawn to thy side by the strong
    Constraint of our kinship, and, kinship apart,
    There is none that I hold in a higher regard.

I will prove thee the truth of my words — it is not
In my nature to flatter with blandishing tongue, —
For behold, make known to me what is thy need,
And ne'er shalt thou say that Oceanus failed
As a friend to thee faithful and stedfast.

PROMETHEUS

Ah, what is this? Hast thou too come to gaze
Upon my labours? How didst thou dare forsake
The stream that bears thy name and vaulted caverns
Of self-grown rock, to journey to this land,
The mother of iron? Is it thy wish to see
My state and share the burden of my sorrows?
Then look on him who was the friend of Zeus
And fellow-founder of his tyranny,
In what fell agonies he bends my limbs!

OCEANUS

I see, Prometheus, and I would commend
To thee, so quick of wit, the wisest course.
Prepare to know thyself and change thy ways
Anew, for new the tyrant of the gods.
If with such barbed and bitter words thou criest
Defiance, Zeus, though far from hence enthroned
On high, might hear thee, and thy present host
Of ills would seem no more than child's play then.
Nay, most unhappy, lay aside thy rage
And from misfortune seek deliverance.
Antique, perchance, may seem my counsel to thee:
Yet such, Prometheus, is the penalty
Paid by the arrogance of a lofty tongue.
Unhumbled yet, thou dost not bow to trouble

But to these ills thou hast would others add.
No longer, if thou wouldst be schooled by me,
Wilt thou thus kick against the pricks, aware
That our harsh monarch owes account to none.
And I will now depart and do my best
To find release from thy adversities.
But hold thy peace and curb thy turbulent speech;
Or, over-subtle, hast thou not wit to see
A price is set upon an idle tongue?

PROMETHEUS

I count thee happy to be free from blame,
Though in my perils all participant.
And now have done, take no concern for me.
Thou canst not move him — he is immovable, —
And watch that no misfortune waylay *thee*.

OCEANUS

Ay, thou wast born to teach thy neighbours wisdom
But not thyself — thy works are proof of that.
Yet, since I have the will, oppose me not.
For I declare that Zeus will grant to me
This favour and release thee from thy pains.

PROMETHEUS

So far I praise thee, and praise thee ever shall —
Thy willingness lacks nothing. Even so
Spare thyself trouble, for labour spent on me
Will yield no profit, despite thy will to spend it.
So, hold thy peace, beyond the reach of harm.
    For I, though ill my fortune, would not seek
Relief in the distress of others too.

Indeed not so; for even now I mourn
My brother Atlas, who in the far west
Bears on his shoulders in no tender clasp
The massive pillar of the Earth and Heaven.
And the earth-born inmate of Cilicia's caves
I saw likewise and pitied, monster dread,
The hundred-headed Typho, as he fell
Subdued, a god who stood against the gods,
Hissing forth terror from his horrid jaws
And from his eyes darting disastrous fire
In challenge to the tyranny of Zeus,
Till on him fell the Lord's unslumbering bolt,
The swift-descending lightning-blast of heaven,
Which struck him low for all his overbold
And high-mouthed arrogance; pierced to the heart,
His cindered strength was thundered out of him.
And now his limp and outstretched body lies
Beside the passage of the ocean straits
Crushed by the roots of Etna's deep foundations;
Upon whose summit stands Hephaestus' smithy,
Under the rumbling ground, whence yet shall spring
Rivers of fire with ravenous jaws devouring
The level fields of fruitful Sicily:
Such are the shafts that Typho's buried wrath,
Though turned to ashes by the bolt of Zeus,
Shall hurl in seething cataracts of fire.
    Nay, thou hast seen; there is no need for me
To school thee. Save thyself as thou knowest how,
And I will bear my sufferings until
The heart of Zeus with spleen is surfeited.

OCEANUS

> Hast thou, Prometheus, never learnt that words
> Are the physicians of distempered rage?

PROMETHEUS

> If in due season they assuage the spirit
> And not by force constrict the swollen heart.

OCEANUS

> What is the penalty thou seest prescribed
> For willingness and courage? Teach me that.

PROMETHEUS

> Pains to no purpose and light-headed folly.

OCEANUS

> Then do not seek to cure my malady:
> Prudence, miscounted folly, profits most.

PROMETHEUS

> Indeed the charge of folly would fall on me.

OCEANUS

> Plainly your words would send me home again.

PROMETHEUS

> Let not your tears for me make enmity —

OCEANUS

> With him new-throned in heaven's omnipotence?

PROMETHEUS

> Beware of him, lest thou provoke his wrath.

OCEANUS
>   Thy fate, Prometheus, is my teacher there.

PROMETHEUS
>   Make haste, begone, preserve thy present mind.

OCEANUS
>   To willing ears that word of thine is spoken:
>   For see, my winged horse impatiently
>   Fans the smooth paths of heaven, and travel-tired
>   In his own stall would gladly bend the knee.

CHORUS (*Strophe 1*)
>   I weep for thee, weep for thy hapless fate, Prometheus.
>   From a full eye are the warm fountains of sorrow on a
>   tender cheek descending
>   And its bloom with tears bedewing;
>   For enthroned in dire oppression by his self-appointed
>   edict
>   To the gods of old the lord Zeus doth reveal o'erweening
>   power.

>   *Antistrophe 1*
>   And all the earth lifteth her voice in lamentation,
>   And the mortals who on earth dwell for thy lost splendour
>   lament and mourn thy brethren's
>   Immemorial age of grandeur;
>   And the peoples who inhabit the expanse of holy Asia
>   In thy loud-lamented labours do partake through grief's
>   communion.

Strophe 2
Those who rule the coast of Colchis,
Maids in battle unaffrighted,
Ay, the Scythian swarm that roameth
Earth's far verges around the wide
Waters of Lake Maeotis;

Antistrophe 2
Araby's flower of martial manhood
Who upon Caucasian highlands
Guard their mountain-cradled stronghold,
Host invincible, armed with keen
Spears in the press of battle.

Epode
But one god else in labours have I seen,
In fetters of adamant held,
The Titan Atlas, who with unequalled strength
The massy pillar of the sky
Alone upholds and weeps his hard fate.
The waves of Ocean cry aloud
Falling, full of sighs the deep,
And Hades stirs with subterranean moan;
Yea and the pure river-fountains are poured
In streams of sad compassion.

PROMETHEUS
Think not my silence is enforced by pride
Or obstinacy — by bitterness of heart
To see myself so savagely outraged.

And yet for these new deities who else
Prescribed their powers and privileges but I?
Of that no more, for the tale that I could tell
Is known to you; but hearken to the plight
Of man, in whom, born witless as a babe,
I planted mind and the gift of understanding.
I speak of men with no intent to blame
But to expound my gracious services:
Who first, with eyes to see, did see in vain,
With ears to hear, did hear not, but as shapes
Figured in dreams throughout their mortal span
Confounded all things, knew not how to raise
Brick-woven walls sun-warmed, nor build in wood,
But had their dwelling, like the restless ant,
In sunless nooks of subterranean caves.
No token sure they had of winter's cold,
No herald of the flowery spring or season
Of ripening fruit, but laboured without wit
In all their works, till I revealed the obscure
Risings and settings of the stars of heaven.
Yea, and the art of number, arch-device,
I founded, and the craft of written words,
The world's recorder, mother of the Muse.
I first subdued the wild beasts of the field
To slave in pack and harness and relieve
The mortal labourer of his heaviest toil,
And yoked in chariots, quick to serve the rein,
The horse, prosperity's proud ornament;
And none but I devised the mariner's car
On hempen wing roaming the trackless ocean.
    Such the resources I have found for man,

Yet for myself, alas, have none to bring
From this my present plight deliverance.

CHORUS

Thy plight is cruel indeed: bereft of wit
And like a bad physician falling sick,
Thou dost despair and for thine own disease
Canst find no physic nor medicament.

PROMETHEUS

Nay, hear the rest and thou wilt marvel more,
What cunning arts and artifices I planned.
    Of all the greatest, if a man fell sick,
There was no remedy, nor shredded herb
Nor draught to drink nor ointment, and in default
Of physic their flesh withered, until I
Revealed the blends of gentle medicines
Wherewith they arm themselves against disease.
And many ways of prophecy I ordered,
And first interpreted what must come of dreams
In waking hours, and the obscure import
Of wayside signs and voices I defined,
And taught them to discern the various flight
Of taloned birds, which of them favourable
And which of ill foreboding, and the ways
Of life by each pursued, their mating-seasons,
Their hatreds and their loves one for another;
The entrails too, of what texture and hue
They must appear to please the sight of heaven;
The dappled figure of the gall and liver,
The thigh-bone wrapt in fat and the long chine

I burnt and led man to the riddling art
Of divination; and augury by fire,
For long in darkness hid, I brought to light.
Such help I gave, and more — beneath the earth,
The buried benefits of humanity,
Iron and bronze, silver and gold, who else
Can claim that he revealed to man but I?
None, I know well, unless an idle braggart.
   In these few words learn briefly my whole tale:
Prometheus founded all the arts of man.

CHORUS

Render not aid to man unrighteously,
Neglectful of thine own misfortunes — thus
I have good hope that, from these bonds released,
Thou shalt return to power, the peer of Zeus.

PROMETHEUS

Not so nor yet hath all-determining Fate
Ordained the end, but, when ten thousand pains
Have crushed my body, from bonds shall I escape.
For Art is weaker than Necessity.

CHORUS

Who then is helmsman of Necessity?

PROMETHEUS

The Fates three-formed and the remembering Furies.

CHORUS

Is Zeus himself less powerful than these?

PROMETHEUS

He could not alter that which is ordained.

CHORUS
> What *is* ordained for Zeus save power eternal?

PROMETHEUS
> Question no more — I will not answer that.

CHORUS
> Some solemn secret doth thy heart embrace.

PROMETHEUS
> Nay, turn to other things — I must not yet
> Make *that* tale manifest, but keep it veiled
> Most jealously — by guarding that shall I
> From these fell bonds and agonies escape.

CHORUS (*Strophe 1*)
> Ne'er may the Ruler of all, Zeus, athwart my purpose array
>   his supreme power,
> Ne'er may I be slow to present to the gods burnt-offerings
>   tended with prayer
> Nigh my father's waters, the slumberless stream which
>   faileth not;
> Ne'er may I sin with my lips — may this prayer abide with
>   me and ne'er within me perish!

> *Antistrophe 1*
> Happy is he who doth pass length of life in sureness of hope
>   and doth feed his
> Heart on gladness sprung from a conscience clear: for truly
>   I shudder as I
> View the thousand sufferings fated for thee. Almighty Zeus

Dauntlessly hast thou defied, ay with froward purpose
 prized mankind too high, Prometheus.

Strophe 2
What reward for thy favours, and where is there succour at
 hand to save thee
In the things of a day? Or have thine eyes not seen how
In a vain, unavailing, dreamlike impotence the purblind
 peoples
Of the earth are imprisoned eternally? Ne'er shall the
Harmony ordered of Zeus be turned awry by mortal coun-
 sels.

Antistrophe 2
Thus indeed am I taught by the sight of thy hapless fate,
 Prometheus.
For alas! unalike the song that now I sing thee
To the tune that of old around thy bridal bath and bed was
 chanted,
As thou camest with gifts to my father to win from him
Beautiful Hesione for thy marriage-bed, a bride to sleep
 beside thee.

(*Enter* IO, *horned like a cow*)

IO

 What people and place is this? whom do I see
 Bridled in boulders and harnessed in stone,
 Laid bare to the storm?
 What offence hath condemned thee to such bitter pain?

O declare to me, where
In the world have my wanderings borne me?

Ah, ah!
Again the gadfly's sting—unhappy maiden!
The ghost of earth-born Argus wakes again.
I see the Herdsman hundred-eyed approach me.
Ever he follows, fixed on me his crafty eye;
Whom even after death the earth conceals not.
Ever he tracks me down out of the land of death,
He hunts me hungry, far astray, hapless wanderer on
   sand-strewn shores.

Strophe
Ever the sleepy music is around my ears,
Melody shrill whispered on waxen reed.
Alas, where, alas,
Where do these wand'rings lead, wanderings aimless, wild?
How have I, O Cronian King,
How have I given offence that I am maltreated so, bound
   and yoked fast to these miseries, woe is me!
What cause hast thou to madden a helpless maid
With terror of goading torment?
Give me to flames to burn, bury me underground,
Ay, to sea-monsters cast my flesh.
Grudge me not, I pray thee, grant my prayer, O king!
Enough my restless wanderings,
I can no more endure, and know not where to find
Respite from this anguish.
The cow-horned maid cries to thee: hear her cry!

PROMETHEUS

> I hear indeed the gadfly-hunted maid,
> Daughter of Inachus, who fired the heart
> Of Zeus with love, and now by Hera's hate
> Is doomed to run her lengthy race of pain.

IO (*Antistrophe*)

> How dost thou know to call me by my father's name?
> Tell me, speak to an unhappy maid,
> Who art thou, hapless one,
> Quick to greet me by my true name with knowledge sure
> Of the distemper heaven-sent to waste my limbs, pangs that
>   spur feet afar wandering, woe is me!
> Distraught with pain and leaping in frenzy high
> I come, to spiteful Hera's
> Venomous wiles a victim, and I ask, of all
> Evil-starred mortal kind, alas,
> Who hath known such anguish? Nay but tell me true,
> Declare to me what sufferings
> Remain, what physic can assuage my plague —
> Show me, if thou knowest!
> O speak, hear the far-wandering maiden's cry!

PROMETHEUS

> I will tell clearly all thou seek'st to know,
> No riddles weaving, but a plain-told tale,
> Even as 'tis meet to open the lips to friends.
> Thou seest Prometheus, giver of fire to man.

IO

> O common benefactor of mankind,
> Prometheus, why art thou condemned to this?

PROMETHEUS
>Even now I ceased to mourn my own misfortunes.

IO
>Wilt thou not grant the gift I ask of thee?

PROMETHEUS
>Say what thou askest: all shalt thou be told.

IO
>Declare who prisoned thee in this rocky glen.

PROMETHEUS
>The will of Zeus worked by Hephaestus' hand.

IO
>Of what offence is this the penalty?

PROMETHEUS
>If I reveal so much, that will suffice.

IO
>Nay, show me also when shall I behold
>The term of my unhappy wanderings.

PROMETHEUS
>Better remain in ignorance of that.

IO
>O hide not from me that which I must suffer!

PROMETHEUS
>'Tis not that I am jealous of the gift.

IO
>Then why so loth to make all manifest?

PROMETHEUS

    I grudge it not, but fear to break thy heart.

IO

    Nay, spare me not against my own desire.

PROMETHEUS

    Since thou dost wish it, I must speak. Attend.

CHORUS

    Not yet: to me likewise vouchsafe a favour.
    First let us learn her malady and hear
    The tale of her wild wanderings, before
    She learns from thee what agonies yet remain.

PROMETHEUS

    Io, thy task it is to grant them this.
    Remember, too, they are thy father's sisters,
    And to bemoan the bitterness of fortune
    To listeners who are like to be moved
    To weep with thee, is labour worth the pains.

IO

    I know not how I can deny your wish:
    All that you seek to know shall in plain words
    Be told. And yet I blush even to recall
    How I, unhappy girl, was seized by that
    Tempest from heaven and beauty's swift decay.
      Night after night dream-visions haunting me
    Came to my chamber and beguiled me thus
    With winning words: O greatly blessed maid,
    Wherefore so long a virgin, when 'tis thine
    To wed the Highest? Zeus with sharp desire

Of thee is smitten and longs for the embrace
Of Cypris. O my child, do not disdain
The bed of Zeus, but get thee to the deep
Meadows of Lerna, thy father's pasturage,
That there the eye of Zeus may ease desire.

   Such were the dreams that each night restlessly
Beset and troubled me, until I dared
To tell my father of those night-fantasies.
Then he sent forth his wise interpreters
To Pytho and Dodona's oaks, to enquire
What might be said or done to please the gods.
With dimly-worded messages they returned,
Obscure reports of dark significance,
Till Inachus received at last a clear
Reply enjoining on him this command,
That he must drive me out from hearth and home
To wander to the confines of the earth,
And, if he disobeyed, the bolt of Zeus
Would visit him, destroying all his house.

   Such were the oracles of Loxias,
And he, as they commanded, cast me forth
Against his will and mine, constrained to do
That which he would not by the curb of Zeus.
Then suddenly, my wit and woman's form
Distorted, with horned temples, as you see,
I sped distraught to the Cerchnean streams
And springs of Lerna, savagely pursued
By Argus, the fierce earth-born Herdsman, who
Kept watch upon me with his hundred eyes,
Till wing-swift death, descending unawares,
Did cut him off; but, gadfly-hunted, I

Before God's scourge still flee across the world.
    Such is my story, and, if thou canst tell
What yet awaits me, speak, and let not pity
Temper the true with false, for I abhor
Above all plagues the tale compact of lies.

CHORUS

    O horrible!
Words so strange, words so full of fear
I never dreamed would come to beat against my ears,
Terror and torture, a sight that doth wound the eye,
Smite my soul with scourging anguish.
Alas, O Fate, Fate, I shudder
With fear to behold the state of Io.

PROMETHEUS

    Too soon thou criest, thy heart surcharged with fear.
Keep back thy tears till thou hast learnt the rest.

CHORUS

    Speak, teach us all: to those who are in sickness
Foreknowledge of their suffering brings relief.

PROMETHEUS

    Your first request you have obtained of me
With ease; for first from her you sought to hear
The unhappy tale of her past sufferings.
Now hear what is to come, what agonies
This young girl must endure from Hera yet.
And thou, O seed of Inachus, lay to heart
What I shall tell, and learn thy journey's end.
    First turn thy face towards the rising sun

Across the unploughed meadow-lands, until
Thou com'st unto the Scythians, wanderers
Who dwell on wheels in wicker chariots,
Armed with far-flying shafts of archery.
Approach not these, but, skirting the long strand
Beside the moaning ocean-surf, pass on
Till on thy left hand thou shalt find the tribe
Of Chalybs, iron-craftsmen, whom beware,
A savage people and inhospitable.
And thou shalt come to the Violent Stream, well-named,
Whose swollen flood must not be forded till
The highest top of Caucasus confront
Thy gaze, from whence that river pours his strength
Sheer from the summit; then, the star-neighbouring peaks
Behind thee, turn thy steps towards the south,
Till thou shalt come unto the Amazons,
Man-hating people, who in Themiscyra
Shall dwell beside Thermodon, by the rock
Of rugged Salmydessus, whose welcome waits
The fearful seaman, stepmother to ships.
And they will gladly lead thee on thy way,
Till at the gateways of the lake thou comest
To the Cimmerian Isthmus, whence pass on
And with stout heart tread the Maeotic Sea.
And of that passage shall mankind relate
The wondrous tale for ever, and shall name
Those waters Bosporus in thy memory.
Thence, leaving Europe, thou shalt come unto
The land of Asia.
   (*To Chorus*) Is it plain to you
The tyrant of the gods is violent

In all his ways? A god, lusting to lie
With mortal woman, he persecutes her thus.
A brutal lover seeks thy hand, my child;
For that which I have now revealed hath scarce
Opened the prelude of thy agony.

CHORUS

Oh me, alas!

PROMETHEUS

Again that cry of pain! What wilt thou do
When thou hast heard the sorrows that remain?

CHORUS

Are further sufferings in store for her?

PROMETHEUS

Ay, a tempestuous sea of misery.

IO

What profit then to live? Let me in haste
Cast myself down from yonder dizzy height,
And buy with one swift leap deliverance
From all my labours! Once to die is better
Than length of days in sorrow without end.

PROMETHEUS

How ill wouldst thou endure *my* sufferings,
Who am by Fate appointed not to die.
That were indeed deliverance from pain,
But for my labours now there is no date
Decreed till Zeus from tyranny hath fallen.

IO

What, can it be the power of Zeus shall fail?

PROMETHEUS

> Glad wouldst thou be, I think, to see that day.

IO

> And who would not, whom Zeus made suffer so?

PROMETHEUS

> Then be assured that it shall come to pass.

IO

> But who shall strip his tyrant sceptre from him?

PROMETHEUS

> Himself by his own empty-headed counsels.

IO

> But how? Declare, if 'tis no harm to tell.

PROMETHEUS

> A marriage shall he make which he will rue.

IO

> Divine or mortal? If 'tis lawful, speak!

PROMETHEUS

> What matter? 'Tis not lawful to say more.

IO

> A bride of his shall cast him from his throne?

PROMETHEUS

> A son shall she bear stronger than his sire.

IO

> And from this destiny has he no escape?

PROMETHEUS

> None, save myself, freed from captivity.

Io

> Who shall deliver thee in despite of Zeus?

PROMETHEUS

> One of thine own descendants shall it be.

Io

> What, shall a son of mine deliver thee?

PROMETHEUS

> The tenth generation and three besides.

Io

> Hard to interpret is that prophecy.

PROMETHEUS

> And of thine own pains seek to learn no more.

Io

> Do not first promise, then withhold, thy gift.

PROMETHEUS

> Two gifts I offer: one or other choose.

Io

> What are they? Speak, that I may make my choice.

PROMETHEUS

> Resolve which thou wouldst hear expounded thee —
> Thy future trials, or my deliverer.

CHORUS

> Nay, grant to her one favour, and accord
> To us the other. Do not grudge the tale:

To her, her future path make manifest,
Declare to us thine own deliverer.

PROMETHEUS
        Since you desire it, I will not refuse
        To manifest all that you seek to know.
        First, Io, learn thy tearful wanderings
        And write them on the tables of thy heart.
           Having passed the stream that parts two continents,
        Take the bright paths trod by the rising sun
        Beside the roar of ocean, until thou come
        To the plains Gorgonian of Cisthene, where
        Dwell the ancient hags, daughters of Phorcys three,
        Swanlike in shape, sharing one common eye,
        One-toothed, on whom the sun hath never shed
        His radiant beam nor the night-wandering moon;
        And near them their three sisters, clothed in wings,
        The serpent-cinctured Gorgons, foes of man,
        On whom no mortal e'er shall look and live.
        Such is the prelude to thy pilgrimage.
        And now to another fearful sight give ear:
        Beware the savage, sharp-mouthed hounds of Zeus,
        The griffins, and the one-eyed thievish host
        Of Arimaspian horsemen, who beside
        The banks of Pluto's golden river dwell.
        Approach not these, but at the ends of earth
        Seek out the swarthy tribesmen who abide
        At the Sun's fount by the brook of Ethiop,
        Along whose verges journey till thou come
        To the cataract where from the Bybline Hills
        Are spilt the holy waters of the Nile,

Leading thee on to that three-cornered land,
Nilotis, where thou, Io, and thy sons
Shall found at last a far-off colony.
    If there is aught in this of dark import,
Repeat your questions, till the tale is clear.
I have much leisure, more than I desire.

CHORUS

If aught remain, passed over or to come,
Of her unhappy wanderings, speak on.
If all hath been made manifest, vouchsafe
My share in that which thou hast promised us.

PROMETHEUS

The end of all her travels she hath heard;
But, lest she should misdoubt my prophecy,
What she endured before her coming hither
I will relate, to prove my story true.
    The bulk of that long tale I will pass over
And to thy latter wanderings proceed.
When thou didst walk the wide Molossian plains,
Even to the lofty ridges of Dodona, where
Thesprotian Zeus holds his prophetic seat
And stands the marvel of the Speaking Oaks,
By whom in plain and unambiguous words
Thou wast proclaimed the glorious Bride Elect
Of Zeus — Ah, is thy memory touched by that? —
Then, gadfly-hunted down the long sea-shore,
Thou didst press on to the Gulf of Rhea, whence
Upon thy tracks the tempest beat thee back;
Wherefore, in time to come, that hollow sea,

Believe me, shall be called Ionian
By all mankind in memory of thy passage.
   Accept this testimony of my understanding,
That it perceives more than the eye beholds.
And now the rest will I reveal to all,
My steps retracing to my former tale.
   A city stands, Canobus, at the extreme
Of Egypt, on the silted mouth of Nile;
And there shall Zeus, thy wits restoring with
A touch, lay on thee his unfearful hand;
And, of that touch begot, thereafter named,
Thou shalt bear swarthy Epaphus, who shall till
The wide lands watered by the spacious Nile.
His fifty children, fifth in descent from him,
Against their will to Argos shall return,
A band of maidens, fleeing from the bed
Of fifty cousins, who with hearts astir,
Hawks after doves, in hot pursuit shall follow,
Unrighteous huntsmen, coveting a match
Unlawful, to be cut off by jealous heaven.
For Pelasgia shall welcome them with deeds
Of blood by woman dared in the dark of night:
Each bride shall rob each bridegroom of his breath,
Steeping in slaughter the dagger's double blade.
Thus may the Cyprian greet *my* enemies!
One daughter only, softened by desire,
Her hand shall hold and blunt the edge of her
Resolve, electing rather to endure
The taunt of coward than of murderess;
And she shall bear a race of kings in Argos.
Too long it were to trace the tale in full,

But from her seed at last shall spring a brave
And glorious Archer, who from bondage shall
Deliver me!
                    Such is the oracle
My age-old Mother, Titan Themis, spake.
So shall it be, but how, 't would take me long
To tell, and thee to hear would profit not.

Io

Eleleu! eleleu!
Yet again is my mind set aflame by the scourge
Of the maddening goad, and the arrow unforged
Driveth me onward;
And my heart is a-plunging with fear in my breast,
And my eyes to and fro wildly are glancing,
And distracted I veer far out of my course
On the wind of my frenzy, unbridled my tongue,
And a torrent of speech falls broken upon
Irresistible waves of disaster.   (*Exit*)

CHORUS (*Strophe 1*)
Wise in exceeding wisdom
He who first did weigh in his heart and declare this saying
        in speech to his neighbours:
Blest are they who seek not a marriage above their own
        degree;
May not the meek and lowly aspire to the hand
Full of gold and exalted in riches, or seek
Wedlock with the nobles of the world.

Antistrophe 1
Ne'er may it fall to my lot, O
Fate all things fulfilling, to be called to the bed of Zeus as
    the bride of the Highest;
Ne'er may I by lords of the heavenly host be woo'd or won;
I tremble ev'n to look on the maiden who hates
Her Olympian wooer, destined to wander in pain
Far and wide, pursued by Hera's jealous rage.

Epode
For me, when even-matched the union,
Naught is there to fear, but only
Ne'er may god above let fall love's glance upon me!
O helpless agony, fruitful in fruitless tears!
What the end might be I know not.
Yea, the plan that Zeus designs
None shall avail to alter.

PROMETHEUS
    And yet shall Zeus, so obstinate of spirit,
    Be humbled, such a marriage will he make
    Which shall o'erthrow him from his tyranny's
    Celestial seat for ever; and then the curse
    His father Cronos uttered as he fell
    From his ancestral throne shall be fulfilled.
    Such is his fate, which to avert can none
    Of all the gods instruct him, only I—
    I know the manner of it. So let him sit
    Proudly exultant in his airy thunders
    And brandishing his bolt of lightning fire;
    For nothing can avail to save him from

Downfall disastrous and dishonourable.
Such is the wrestler he now trains against
Himself, a prodigy unconquerable,
Whose strength shall battle down the lightning blast
And master the mighty roar of heaven's thunder;
And then that brandished spear which plagues the Earth,
The trident of Poseidon, shall be shattered,
And, stumbling upon disaster, Zeus shall learn
How far from sovranty is servitude.

CHORUS

Thy wish has fathered this proud threat to Zeus.

PROMETHEUS

I speak what shall be, likewise what I desire.

CHORUS

Is it possible that Zeus shall serve another?

PROMETHEUS

Yea, and be yoked to harsher pains than *these*.

CHORUS

Hast thou no fear to hurl such menaces?

PROMETHEUS

What should I fear, predestined not to die?

CHORUS

He will devise yet greater anguish for thee.

PROMETHEUS

Then let him do it! All things have I foreseen.

CHORUS

The wise are those who bow to Adrasteia.

PROMETHEUS

> Bow down, adore, cringe on thy present master;
> To me is Zeus a thing of no account.
> Nay, let him reign supreme and work his will
> For his brief day — he shall not rule for long.
>
> But see where comes the courier of Zeus,
> The lackey of the new tyrant of the gods.
> Some news, assuredly, he has to tell.

HERMES

> Thou, cunning wit, outbittering bitterness,
> Who gave to creatures of a day the gods'
> High privileges, thee, thief of fire, I call.
> The Father bids thee instantly reveal
> This vaunted marriage, whate'er it be, whereby
> His power shall fail, and that not riddlingly
> But clear in each particular, and so spare me
> A second journey; for thou seest, Prometheus,
> The heart of Zeus is softened not by this.

PROMETHEUS

> How solemn-mouthed and puffed with arrogance
> The announcement, as befits a gods' attendant!
> New, new are you to power, and yet you think
> Your citadel is impregnable. Have I not seen
> Two tyrants cast already from their thrones? —
> Ay, and shall see the third, your present sovran,
> In shame hurled headlong: and dost thou think that I
> In fear of these new gods will cower and quake?
> Far, far am I from that. And, as for thee,

> Begone, retrace the path that brought thee hither;
> For thou shalt learn nothing thou seek'st to know.

HERMES

> Such was the obstinate spirit which called down
> Thy present calamities upon thy head.

PROMETHEUS

> I have no wish to change my adverse fortune,
> Be well assured, for thy subservience.

HERMES

> Better indeed to wait upon this rock
> Than serve as trusted minister of Zeus.

PROMETHEUS

> Such arrogance befits the arrogant.

HERMES

> In thy present state, it seems, thou dost exult.

PROMETHEUS

> Exult! May I behold my enemies
> Exulting so, and thee I count among them.

HERMES

> What, dost thou blame me also for thy plight?

PROMETHEUS

> In simple truth, all of the gods I hate,
> Who, served by me so well, maltreat me thus.

HERMES

> 'Tis plain, most sorely is thy mind diseased.

PROMETHEUS

> Is hate of enemies sickness? Then heal me not.

HERMES
>Thou wouldst be insufferable in prosperity.

PROMETHEUS
>Ah me!

HERMES
>Ah me! That is a cry unknown to Zeus.

PROMETHEUS
>Yet all is being taught by aging Time.

HERMES
>Ay, *thou* hast yet to learn a wiser mind.

PROMETHEUS
>True, or I'd not have spoken to a slave.

HERMES
>Thou wilt not grant, then, what the Father asks.

PROMETHEUS
>I would repay him if I owed him aught.

HERMES
>Thou hast reviled me as though I were a child.

PROMETHEUS
>And art thou not more simple than a child
>If thou dost hope to learn one jot from me?
>No rack nor pillory can Zeus devise
>To move me to make manifest these things
>Till he release me from these insolent bonds.
>So, let him hurl his sulphurous flames from heaven,
>With white-winged snow and subterranean thunder

Make chaos and confusion of the world!
Not thus will he constrain my tongue to tell
By whose hand he from tyranny shall fall.

HERMES

Take thought, consider, art thou helped by this?

PROMETHEUS

These things were seen and thought on long ago.

HERMES

Nay, bring thyself, infatuate, to learn
From this thy present state a sounder mind.

PROMETHEUS

'Tis vain, thy words might sooner stem the waves.
Or dost thou deem that I, fearing the purpose
Of Zeus, will, woman-hearted, supplicate
My hated adversary with bow abased
And abject inclination of my palms,
To free me from my bondage? It cannot be.

HERMES

Much to no purpose have I said, it seems.
Unmelted art thou yet nor softened by
My prayers, but, like a newly-bridled colt,
Dost champ and chafe against the irksome rein.
Yet the conceit that gives thee strength is frail:
For obstinacy, sustained not by a mind
Of healthy judgment, has no strength at all.
　　Consider, if thou wilt not hearken to me,
What dreadful tempest and wild waves of woe
Will overwhelm thee. First, this icy cliff

The Father's thunder-clap and lightning-flame
Shall blast asunder, and thy body, clasped
In the rock's embrace, bury beneath the earth:
Till, having outlived an endless expanse of Time,
Thou shalt return to light, and then the hound
Of Zeus, the blood-red eagle, ravenously
Shall tear thy tattered body limb from limb,
An uninvited, day-long banqueter
Feasting upon thy liver's blackened flesh.
Such woe awaits thee, whereto expect no end
Until some god appear, relieving thee
Of toil, content to face the lightless glooms
Of Hades and the pit of Tartarus.
    Even so take counsel with thyself, for this
Is no fictitious menace, but too true:
To speak false is unknown to the mouth of Zeus,
Each word shall be accomplished. So then, do you
Take heed, deliberate, and do not hold
Good counsel cheaper than an obstinate spirit.

CHORUS

To us it seems that Hermes speaks in season,
Bidding thee lay aside thy obstinacy
And with good counsel walk the path of wisdom.
Yield! It is baseness for the wise to err.

PROMETHEUS

Known to me, known was the message that he
Hath proclaimed, and for none is it shameful to bear
At the hands of his enemies evil and wrong.
So now let him cast, if it please him, the two-

Edged curl of his lightning, and shatter the sky
With his thundering frenzy of furious winds;
Let the earth be uptorn from her roots by the storm
Of his anger, and Ocean with turbulent tides
Pile up, till engulfed are the paths of the stars;
Down to the bottomless blackness of Tartarus
Let my body be cast, caught in the whirling
Waters of Destiny:
For with death *I* shall not be stricken!

HERMES

Nay, such are the feverish cries of a mind
Distorted, the crazed counsels of madmen.
What but the depth of distraction that desperate
Boast? what sign yet that his fury abates?
Be it so; and do you, who have come to his side
In compassion, begone, make good your escape,
That you may not be struck down senseless and stunned
By the roar of the thunder of heaven.

CHORUS

To a different tune must thou speak to persuade;
That turbulent threat is beyond sufferance.
Wouldst thou have me a coward, betraying a friend?
What he must I am willing to bear at his side.
For disloyalty I have been taught to detest —
The disease above all
That repels me with hatred and loathing.

HERMES

Be it so, but remember I warned you away,
Nor, embroiled in the meshes of ruin, complain

Of your fortune, nor feign that unwarned, unawares
Zeus suddenly smote you, but blame yourselves:
Yea, wittingly, willingly, folly-beguiled,
Will your feet be entrapped
In the far-flung nets of disaster!

PROMETHEUS

O mark, no longer in word but in deed,
Earth has been shaken;
The reverberant thunder is heard from the deep,
And the forked flame flares of the lightning, the coiled
Dust flieth upward, the four winds are at play
Frolicking wildly in ruin and riot,
And the sky and the sea in confusion are one:
Such is the storm Zeus gathers against me,
Ever nearer approaching with terrible tread.
O majestical Mother, O heavenly Sky,
In whose region revolveth the Light of the World,
Thou seest the wrongs that I suffer!

DOVER·THRIFT·EDITIONS

POETRY

GUNGA DIN AND OTHER FAVORITE POEMS, Rudyard Kipling. 80pp. 26471-8

SNAKE AND OTHER POEMS, D. H. Lawrence. 64pp. 40647-4

THE CONGO AND OTHER POEMS, Vachel Lindsay. 96pp. 27272-9

EVANGELINE AND OTHER POEMS, Henry Wadsworth Longfellow. 64pp. 28255-4

FAVORITE POEMS, Henry Wadsworth Longfellow. 96pp. 27273-7

"TO HIS COY MISTRESS" AND OTHER POEMS, Andrew Marvell. 64pp. 29544-3

SPOON RIVER ANTHOLOGY, Edgar Lee Masters. 144pp. 27275-3

SELECTED POEMS, Claude McKay. 80pp. 40876-0

RENASCENCE AND OTHER POEMS, Edna St. Vincent Millay. 64pp. (Available in U.S. only.) 26873-X

SELECTED POEMS, John Milton. 128pp. 27554-X

CIVIL WAR POETRY: An Anthology, Paul Negri (ed.). 128pp. 29883-3

ENGLISH VICTORIAN POETRY: AN ANTHOLOGY, Paul Negri (ed.). 256pp. 40425-0

GREAT SONNETS, Paul Negri (ed.). 96pp. 28052-7

THE RAVEN AND OTHER FAVORITE POEMS, Edgar Allan Poe. 64pp. 26685-0

ESSAY ON MAN AND OTHER POEMS, Alexander Pope. 128pp. 28053-5

EARLY POEMS, Ezra Pound. 80pp. (Available in U.S. only.) 28745-9

GREAT POEMS BY AMERICAN WOMEN: An Anthology, Susan L. Rattiner (ed.). 224pp. (Available in U.S. only.) 40164-2

LITTLE ORPHANT ANNIE AND OTHER POEMS, James Whitcomb Riley. 80pp. 28260-0

GOBLIN MARKET AND OTHER POEMS, Christina Rossetti. 64pp. 28055-1

CHICAGO POEMS, Carl Sandburg. 80pp. 28057-8

CORNHUSKERS, Carl Sandburg. 157pp. 41409-4

THE SHOOTING OF DAN MCGREW AND OTHER POEMS, Robert Service. 96pp. (Available in U.S. only.) 27556-6

COMPLETE SONNETS, William Shakespeare. 80pp. 26686-9

SELECTED POEMS, Percy Bysshe Shelley. 128pp. 27558-2

AFRICAN-AMERICAN POETRY: An Anthology, 1773–1930, Joan R. Sherman (ed.). 96pp. 29604-0

100 BEST-LOVED POEMS, Philip Smith (ed.). 96pp. 28553-7

NATIVE AMERICAN SONGS AND POEMS: An Anthology, Brian Swann (ed.). 64pp. 29450-1

SELECTED POEMS, Alfred Lord Tennyson. 112pp. 27282-6

AENEID, Vergil (Publius Vergilius Maro). 256pp. 28749-1

CHRISTMAS CAROLS: COMPLETE VERSES, Shane Weller (ed.). 64pp. 27397-0

GREAT LOVE POEMS, Shane Weller (ed.). 128pp. 27284-2

CIVIL WAR POETRY AND PROSE, Walt Whitman. 96pp. 28507-3

SELECTED POEMS, Walt Whitman. 128pp. 26878-0

THE BALLAD OF READING GAOL AND OTHER POEMS, Oscar Wilde. 64pp. 27072-6

EARLY POEMS, William Carlos Williams. 64pp. (Available in U.S. only.) 29294-0

FAVORITE POEMS, William Wordsworth. 80pp. 27073-4

WORLD WAR ONE BRITISH POETS: Brooke, Owen, Sassoon, Rosenberg, and Others, Candace Ward (ed.). (Available in U.S. only.) 29568-0

EARLY POEMS, William Butler Yeats. 128pp. 27808-5

"EASTER, 1916" AND OTHER POEMS, William Butler Yeats. 80pp. (Available in U.S. only.) 29771-3

DOVER · THRIFT · EDITIONS

FICTION

FLATLAND: A ROMANCE OF MANY DIMENSIONS, Edwin A. Abbott. 96pp. 27263-X

SHORT STORIES, Louisa May Alcott. 64pp. 29063-8

WINESBURG, OHIO, Sherwood Anderson. 160pp. 28269-4

PERSUASION, Jane Austen. 224pp. 29555-9

PRIDE AND PREJUDICE, Jane Austen. 272pp. 28473-5

SENSE AND SENSIBILITY, Jane Austen. 272pp. 29049-2

LOOKING BACKWARD, Edward Bellamy. 160pp. 29038-7

BEOWULF, Beowulf (trans. by R. K. Gordon). 64pp. 27264-8

CIVIL WAR STORIES, Ambrose Bierce. 128pp. 28038-1

"THE MOONLIT ROAD" AND OTHER GHOST AND HORROR STORIES, Ambrose Bierce (John Grafton, ed.) 96pp. 40056-5

WUTHERING HEIGHTS, Emily Brontë. 256pp. 29256-8

THE THIRTY-NINE STEPS, John Buchan. 96pp. 28201-5

TARZAN OF THE APES, Edgar Rice Burroughs. 224pp. (Available in U.S. only.) 29570-2

ALICE'S ADVENTURES IN WONDERLAND, Lewis Carroll. 96pp. 27543-4

THROUGH THE LOOKING-GLASS, Lewis Carroll. 128pp. 40878-7

MY ÁNTONIA, Willa Cather. 176pp. 28240-6

O PIONEERS!, Willa Cather. 128pp. 27785-2

PAUL'S CASE AND OTHER STORIES, Willa Cather. 64pp. 29057-3

FIVE GREAT SHORT STORIES, Anton Chekhov. 96pp. 26463-7

TALES OF CONJURE AND THE COLOR LINE, Charles Waddell Chesnutt. 128pp. 40426-9

FAVORITE FATHER BROWN STORIES, G. K. Chesterton. 96pp. 27545-0

THE AWAKENING, Kate Chopin. 128pp. 27786-0

A PAIR OF SILK STOCKINGS AND OTHER STORIES, Kate Chopin. 64pp. 29264-9

HEART OF DARKNESS, Joseph Conrad. 80pp. 26464-5

LORD JIM, Joseph Conrad. 256pp. 40650-4

THE SECRET SHARER AND OTHER STORIES, Joseph Conrad. 128pp. 27546-9

THE "LITTLE REGIMENT" AND OTHER CIVIL WAR STORIES, Stephen Crane. 80pp. 29557-5

THE OPEN BOAT AND OTHER STORIES, Stephen Crane. 128pp. 27547-7

THE RED BADGE OF COURAGE, Stephen Crane. 112pp. 26465-3

MOLL FLANDERS, Daniel Defoe. 256pp. 29093-X

ROBINSON CRUSOE, Daniel Defoe. 288pp. 40427-7

A CHRISTMAS CAROL, Charles Dickens. 80pp. 26865-9

THE CRICKET ON THE HEARTH AND OTHER CHRISTMAS STORIES, Charles Dickens. 128pp. 28039-X

A TALE OF TWO CITIES, Charles Dickens. 304pp. 40651-2

THE DOUBLE, Fyodor Dostoyevsky. 128pp. 29572-9

THE GAMBLER, Fyodor Dostoyevsky. 112pp. 29081-6

NOTES FROM THE UNDERGROUND, Fyodor Dostoyevsky. 96pp. 27053-X

THE ADVENTURE OF THE DANCING MEN AND OTHER STORIES, Sir Arthur Conan Doyle. 80pp. 29558-3

THE HOUND OF THE BASKERVILLES, Arthur Conan Doyle. 128pp. 28214-7

THE LOST WORLD, Arthur Conan Doyle. 176pp. 40060-3

DOVER · THRIFT · EDITIONS

FICTION

SIX GREAT SHERLOCK HOLMES STORIES, Sir Arthur Conan Doyle. 112pp. 27055-6

SHORT STORIES, Theodore Dreiser. 112pp. 28215-5

SILAS MARNER, George Eliot. 160pp. 29246-0

THIS SIDE OF PARADISE, F. Scott Fitzgerald. 208pp. 28999-0

"THE DIAMOND AS BIG AS THE RITZ" AND OTHER STORIES, F. Scott Fitzgerald. 29991-0

MADAME BOVARY, Gustave Flaubert. 256pp. 29257-6

THE REVOLT OF "MOTHER" AND OTHER STORIES, Mary E. Wilkins Freeman. 128pp. 40428-5

A ROOM WITH A VIEW, E. M. Forster. 176pp. (Available in U.S. only.) 28467-0

WHERE ANGELS FEAR TO TREAD, E. M. Forster. 128pp. (Available in U.S. only.) 27791-7

THE IMMORALIST, André Gide. 112pp. (Available in U.S. only.) 29237-1

HERLAND, Charlotte Perkins Gilman. 128pp. 40429-3

"THE YELLOW WALLPAPER" AND OTHER STORIES, Charlotte Perkins Gilman. 80pp. 29857-4

THE OVERCOAT AND OTHER STORIES, Nikolai Gogol. 112pp. 27057-2

CHELKASH AND OTHER STORIES, Maxim Gorky. 64pp. 40652-0

GREAT GHOST STORIES, John Grafton (ed.). 112pp. 27270-2

DETECTION BY GASLIGHT, Douglas G. Greene (ed.). 272pp. 29928-7

THE MABINOGION, Lady Charlotte E. Guest. 192pp. 29541-9

"THE FIDDLER OF THE REELS" AND OTHER SHORT STORIES, Thomas Hardy. 80pp. 29960-0

THE LUCK OF ROARING CAMP AND OTHER STORIES, Bret Harte. 96pp. 27271-0

THE HOUSE OF THE SEVEN GABLES, Nathaniel Hawthorne. 272pp. 40882-5

THE SCARLET LETTER, Nathaniel Hawthorne. 192pp. 28048-9

YOUNG GOODMAN BROWN AND OTHER STORIES, Nathaniel Hawthorne. 128pp. 27060-2

THE GIFT OF THE MAGI AND OTHER SHORT STORIES, O. Henry. 96pp. 27061-0

THE NUTCRACKER AND THE GOLDEN POT, E. T. A. Hoffmann. 128pp. 27806-9

THE BEAST IN THE JUNGLE AND OTHER STORIES, Henry James. 128pp. 27552-3

DAISY MILLER, Henry James. 64pp. 28773-4

THE TURN OF THE SCREW, Henry James. 96pp. 26684-2

WASHINGTON SQUARE, Henry James. 176pp. 40431-5

THE COUNTRY OF THE POINTED FIRS, Sarah Orne Jewett. 96pp. 28196-5

THE AUTOBIOGRAPHY OF AN EX-COLORED MAN, James Weldon Johnson. 112pp. 28512-X

DUBLINERS, James Joyce. 160pp. 26870-5

A PORTRAIT OF THE ARTIST AS A YOUNG MAN, James Joyce. 192pp. 28050-0

THE METAMORPHOSIS AND OTHER STORIES, Franz Kafka. 96pp. 29030-1

THE MAN WHO WOULD BE KING AND OTHER STORIES, Rudyard Kipling. 128pp. 28051-9

YOU KNOW ME AL, Ring Lardner. 128pp. 28513-8

SELECTED SHORT STORIES, D. H. Lawrence. 128pp. 27794-1

GREEN TEA AND OTHER GHOST STORIES, J. Sheridan LeFanu. 96pp. 27795-X

THE CALL OF THE WILD, Jack London. 64pp. 26472-6

FIVE GREAT SHORT STORIES, Jack London. 96pp. 27063-7

THE SEA-WOLF, Jack London. iv+244pp. 41108-7

WHITE FANG, Jack London. 160pp. 26968-X

DEATH IN VENICE, Thomas Mann. 96pp. (Available in U.S. only.) 28714-9

IN A GERMAN PENSION: 13 Stories, Katherine Mansfield. 112pp. 28719-X

DOVER·THRIFT·EDITIONS

FICTION

THE NECKLACE AND OTHER SHORT STORIES, Guy de Maupassant. 128pp. 27064-5
BARTLEBY AND BENITO CERENO, Herman Melville. 112pp. 26473-4
THE OIL JAR AND OTHER STORIES, Luigi Pirandello. 96pp. 28459-X
THE GOLD-BUG AND OTHER TALES, Edgar Allan Poe. 128pp. 26875-6
TALES OF TERROR AND DETECTION, Edgar Allan Poe. 96pp. 28744-0
THE QUEEN OF SPADES AND OTHER STORIES, Alexander Pushkin. 128pp. 28054-3
THE STORY OF AN AFRICAN FARM, Olive Schreiner. 256pp. 40165-0
FRANKENSTEIN, Mary Shelley. 176pp. 28211-2
THREE LIVES, Gertrude Stein. 176pp. (Available in U.S. only.) 28059-4
THE STRANGE CASE OF DR. JEKYLL AND MR. HYDE, Robert Louis Stevenson. 64pp.
   26688-5
TREASURE ISLAND, Robert Louis Stevenson. 160pp. 27559-0
GULLIVER'S TRAVELS, Jonathan Swift. 240pp. 29273-8
THE KREUTZER SONATA AND OTHER SHORT STORIES, Leo Tolstoy. 144pp. 27805-0
THE WARDEN, Anthony Trollope. 176pp. 40076-X
FIRST LOVE AND DIARY OF A SUPERFLUOUS MAN, Ivan Turgenev. 96pp. 28775-0
FATHERS AND SONS, Ivan Turgenev. 176pp. 40073-5
ADVENTURES OF HUCKLEBERRY FINN, Mark Twain. 224pp. 28061-6
THE ADVENTURES OF TOM SAWYER, Mark Twain. 192pp. 40077-8
THE MYSTERIOUS STRANGER AND OTHER STORIES, Mark Twain. 128pp. 27069-6
HUMOROUS STORIES AND SKETCHES, Mark Twain. 80pp. 29279-7
AROUND THE WORLD IN EIGHTY DAYS, Jules Verne. 160pp. 41111-7
CANDIDE, Voltaire (François-Marie Arouet). 112pp. 26689-3
GREAT SHORT STORIES BY AMERICAN WOMEN, Candace Ward (ed.). 192pp. 28776-9
"THE COUNTRY OF THE BLIND" AND OTHER SCIENCE-FICTION STORIES, H. G. Wells. 160pp.
   (Available in U.S. only.) 29569-9
THE ISLAND OF DR. MOREAU, H. G. Wells. 112pp. (Available in U.S. only.) 29027-1
THE INVISIBLE MAN, H. G. Wells. 112pp. (Available in U.S. only.) 27071-8
THE TIME MACHINE, H. G. Wells. 80pp. (Available in U.S. only.) 28472-7
THE WAR OF THE WORLDS, H. G. Wells. 160pp. (Available in U.S. only.) 29506-0
ETHAN FROME, Edith Wharton. 96pp. 26690-7
SHORT STORIES, Edith Wharton. 128pp. 28235-X
THE AGE OF INNOCENCE, Edith Wharton. 288pp. 29803-5
THE PICTURE OF DORIAN GRAY, Oscar Wilde. 192pp. 27807-7
JACOB'S ROOM, Virginia Woolf. 144pp. (Available in U.S. only.) 40109-X
MONDAY OR TUESDAY: Eight Stories, Virginia Woolf. 64pp. (Available in U.S. only.) 29453-6

NONFICTION

POETICS, Aristotle. 64pp. 29577-X
POLITICS, Aristotle. 368pp. 41424-8
NICOMACHEAN ETHICS, Aristotle. 256pp. 40096-4
MEDITATIONS, Marcus Aurelius. 128pp. 29823-X
THE LAND OF LITTLE RAIN, Mary Austin. 96pp. 29037-9
THE DEVIL'S DICTIONARY, Ambrose Bierce. 144pp. 27542-6
THE ANALECTS, Confucius. 128pp. 28484-0
CONFESSIONS OF AN ENGLISH OPIUM EATER, Thomas De Quincey. 80pp. 28742-4
NARRATIVE OF THE LIFE OF FREDERICK DOUGLASS, Frederick Douglass. 96pp. 28499-9